Amelia Bedelia

Dances Off

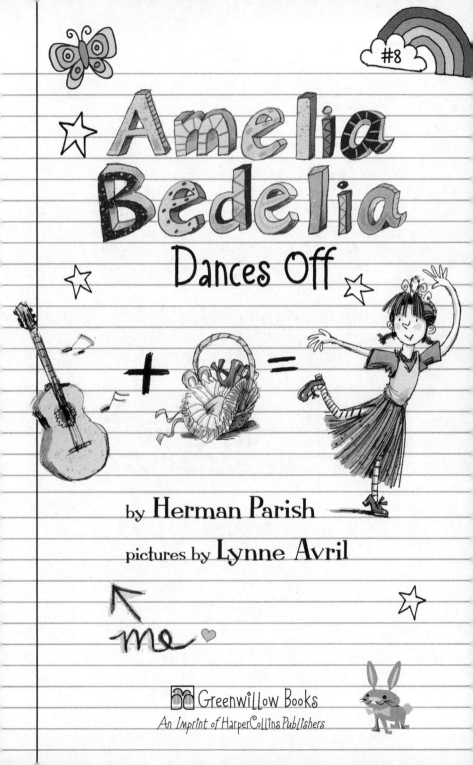

#8

Amelia Bedelia
Dances Off

by Herman Parish

pictures by Lynne Avril

← me ♥

Greenwillow Books
An Imprint of HarperCollins Publishers

Gouache and black pencil were used to prepare the black-and-white art.

Amelia Bedelia is a registered trademark of Peppermint Partners, LLC.

Amelia Bedelia Dances Off. Text copyright © 2015 by Herman S. Parish III. Illustrations copyright © 2015 by
Lynne Avril. All rights reserved. No part of this book may be used or reproduced in any manner whatsoever
without written permission except in the case of brief quotations embodied in critical articles and reviews.
Printed in the United States of America. For information address HarperCollins Children's Books, a division
of HarperCollins Publishers, 195 Broadway, New York, NY 10007. www.harpercollinschildrens.com

Library of Congress Cataloging-in-Publication Data is available.

ISBN 978-0-06-233409-1 (hardback)—ISBN 978-0-06-233408-4 (pbk. ed.)
"Greenwillow Books."

19 20 CG/LSCH 10 9 8 7 6 5 4   First Edition

Greenwillow Books

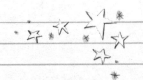

For Susan & Chris Bryan-Brown

Keep dancing! —H. P.

With love to Karen Ninos Carpenter,

My Bunny Ballerina—L. A.

Contents

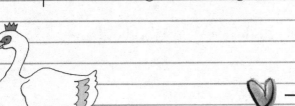

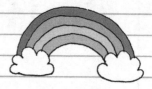

Chapter 1

Wanda Dance?

Amelia Bedelia had been looking forward to this moment all week long. She had finished her homework, made a yummy snack, poured a giant glass of apple juice, and arranged everything on the table next to her father's favorite chair, a recliner covered in soft leather.

This was where he always sat to watch sports on TV and catch up on his sleep. Amelia Bedelia's mother jokingly called the recliner his "throne" because he loved to sit there so much, like a king ruling the kingdom. Amelia Bedelia wouldn't dare sit in her dad's recliner if he were at home. Luckily, he was still at work!

Now, she climbed into it and got comfortable. The recliner actually lived up to its name. Amelia Bedelia thought that was probably why it was her favorite chair too. After all, the armchairs in her house did not have real arms. The footstool did not have any feet. The coffee table was not brown, and it had never made a pot of coffee. It just held magazines. But the recliner really reclined. When she pulled on the handle and snuggled back, a cushion popped up for her feet.

Amelia Bedelia's dog, Finally, put her front paws on the seat and got ready to jump into the recliner too.

"Down, girl!" said Amelia Bedelia. "King Dad would throw us both in the dungeon if he found us here."

Finally walked in a circle three times and settled under the footrest.

"Ahhhhhh!" Amelia Bedelia sighed as she sank back into the soft leather cushion. No wonder her father never wanted to get up. She aimed the remote control at the TV.

Ahhhhh!

"Three, two, one—*blastoff!*" Amelia Bedelia pressed the ON button.

Her timing was perfect. Trumpets blared a fanfare as a deep-voiced announcer declared, "Welcome to this week's episode of *The World Is a Village*."

This was followed by a close-up shot of a hand sticking a pin into a specific spot on a map. Each episode took place in a remote corner of the world that Amelia Bedelia had never studied in geography or even heard of. That was what made it so great. Plus, *The World Is a Village* was popular years ago, and it was so old that sometimes the episode was in black and white instead of color. That didn't matter to her. She just loved learning about the awesome customs and costumes and ceremonies from around the world.

"In these remote rain forests . . . ," said the announcer as the camera panned over tall trees draped in vines, "two tribes celebrate a year of peace by sharing their ceremonial dances." Tall figures in incredible costumes were swaying back and forth. Amelia Bedelia would have given anything to wear a costume like that, even for one day. Drummers were drumming furiously in short, percussive bursts. Amelia Bedelia began drumming on the arms of the recliner. She wanted drums of her own!

POP-Pu-POP! POPPUPOP-Pop-Pop-POP Patta-POP POP POP!"

It sounded so realistic, the drums could have been in the next room.

"Cooks prepare a feast that goes on for days," said the announcer.

"*Mmmmm* . . . honey-dipped grasshoppers, anyone?"

"Yuck!" Amelia Bedelia inhaled sharply. To her surprise, she smelled a delicious aroma. She looked toward the kitchen and there was her mother, coming through the doorway carrying a bowl of popcorn. It had been the percussion section and the feast, all in one.

"Can the princess scoot over and share the throne?" asked her mother. "The queen needs a break."

"Certainly, Your Highness," said Amelia Bedelia, making room for her mom. "Will you

7

share your bounty of popped corn?"

Her mother slid into the recliner next to Amelia Bedelia, and they both grabbed a big handful of popcorn.

"Why is that guy leading a goat around the village?" asked her mother.

"I'm not sure," said Amelia Bedelia. "You were getting into the throne when the announcer was explaining that."

"Is that the chief being carried ahead of the others?" asked her mother.

"I guess so," said Amelia Bedelia.

"How come that beautiful woman has feathers coming out of her armpits?" asked her mother.

"I have no idea," said Amelia Bedelia. "Stop asking questions and listen! Then we'll both find out."

Now she knew why her father got so annoyed with her mother. Her mom had the habit of wandering into the family room and peppering everyone with questions at the exact moment a show was getting good!

Just then, Finally's paws appeared on the footrest.

"Down, girl," said Amelia Bedelia.

But Finally hated to be left out. She jumped onto the recliner.

"Hold on, sweetie!" yelled Amelia Bedelia's mother.

The recliner snapped back and the bowl went flying, showering the family room with popcorn. The recliner had reclined all the way, and now it was a bed. Finally dove for the spilled popcorn, and Amelia Bedelia and her mother began laughing hysterically.

"Shhhh!" her mother said suddenly,

click-A-click, clickty-click clickty-clickty SLACK

putting her fingers to her lips. "What's that noise?" *click-A-click, clickty-click clickty-clickty SLACK*

CLICK-A-CLICK, CLICKTY-CLICK CLICKITY-CLICKTY-CLACK.

"It's part of the show," said Amelia Bedelia. "On the TV."

"No, not that noise," said her mother. "*That* noise."

"Finally, NO!" shouted Amelia Bedelia. Finally was loudly spitting up popcorn and looking pretty sorry for herself. "I guess Finally doesn't like popcorn, Mom."

"No, not that noise," said her mother. "THAT NOISE!" She pointed at the window that faced their front walk. They both slipped off the recliner and crawled

11

through the spilled popcorn to peek out
the window.

"Is that . . . ," said Amelia Bedelia's
mother.

"Aunt Wanda!" yelled Amelia Bedelia,
jumping up. She raced to the front door,
flung it open, ran down the walkway, and
jumped into Aunt Wanda's arms. Wanda

was a large woman, but it had been a while since she had held Amelia Bedelia.

"Easy, easy," said Wanda, laughing. "You've grown since the last time you did that!" She let Amelia Bedelia slip down to the ground and gave Amelia Bedelia's mother a hello hug.

"We're so glad to see you, Wanda," said Amelia Bedelia's mother. "For someone who lives so close by, we don't see enough of you!"

"This is all of Aunt Wanda," said Amelia Bedelia, pointing to her aunt. "Look, Mom."

They both gave Wanda a good look, and that's when they noticed her costume and the shoes.

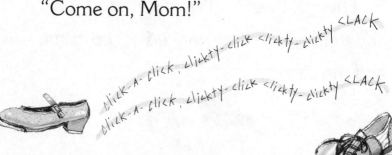

"Are those tap shoes?" asked Amelia Bedelia's mother.

Wanda replied by shuffling her feet. *CLICKTY-CLICK-CLICK-CLACK.* "You bet they are," she said. "I need your help. We've got a state record to set. Come on, my car is waiting."

"State record?" said Amelia Bedelia. "Come on, Mom!"

click-a-click, clickty-click clickty-clickty CLACK
click-a-click, clickty-click clickty-clickty CLACK

Chapter 2

Who's That street Tapping on My ~~Door~~?

"Slow down!" said Amelia Bedelia's mother as Aunt Wanda veered around a curve, tires squealing. "Where are you taking us?"

"To Tepper's Department Store," said Wanda.

"To shop?" asked Amelia Bedelia.

"To shuffle-shuffle-shuffle-shuffle-tap," said Wanda.

Tepper's

Wanda was talking even faster than she drove. Now Amelia Bedelia really understood why her father had nicknamed his big sister "Motor Mouth."

"Every year, they close off the street in front of Tepper's," said Wanda. "How have you missed this? Tap dancers flock from all over for one big tap dance. Hundreds of people show up for Tap into Tepper's, the store's big sale. My friend Dana is in charge of teaching everyone the Tepper routine."

"We don't have tap shoes," said Amelia Bedelia.

"You provide the feet," said Wanda. "I'll provide the shoes."

A parking spot appeared just around

the corner from the store, and Wanda
snagged it. She grabbed a shopping bag
off the backseat.

"Try these on," she said, handing a
pair of tap shoes to Amelia Bedelia and
another pair to her mother. The
pair for her mom was scuffed and
about three sizes too big.

"No problem," said Wanda,
handing two pairs of cotton socks
to Amelia Bedelia's mother. "Put
these on and they'll be snugger.
Those were my first
pair of taps."

Amelia Bedelia's shoes
were brand-new and
fit perfectly.

Happy Birthday!

"Happy birthday," said Wanda.
"This is part one of your gift—just a little bit early!"

Amelia Bedelia reached over the back of the driver's seat and hugged her aunt. "Thank you, Aunt Wanda!" she said.

"No practicing on our hardwood floors, sweetie," said Amelia Bedelia's mother.

The Tepper's tap lesson was just starting. Amelia Bedelia and her mother followed Wanda into the thick of the crowd, which parted for her, until they were on the sidewalk in front of the store. Dana was right above them, standing on a small platform covered with red bunting. Wanda waved at Dana, and Dana waved back.

Dana was wearing a red, white, and blue sequined outfit with a star-spangled scarf tied around her neck. She sported shiny red tap shoes, and she was holding a bullhorn.

"Okay, all you Tepper Tappers!" she yelled. "We're going to learn the simple steps first, so you can all participate. Experienced tappers, help your neighbors! First, take your right foot and tap your toe four times."

She demonstrated the step, and everyone did it together as she counted, "One, two, three, four." Then they did the same thing with their left feet.

"Now," Dana said, "Lift your right heel and tap—one, two, three, four." They sounded better this time. They did the same thing with their left heels.

"You've got it! Now let's try some more toe taps," said Dana.

"heels"

20

"Bend your left knee, letting your right leg slide out. Now tap your right toe on the ground." They did that eight times, then they did the same thing with the other leg.

"brush"

"Wonderful! Now this is called the brush-and-drag," Dana hollered into the bullhorn. "Right foot brush!" When she said the word "brush" they all imitated her, swinging their right feet forward like they were kicking a ball, while skimming their toe taps on the ground. A scratchy metal sound arose from the crowd.

"Now drag," she said, and

"drag"

21

they all swung their right feet back, letting the taps on their heels hit the ground as they did so. They did the sequence seven more times to make sure they had it, then switched to the other foot for another eight brush-and-drags.

"Now let's put it all together," said Dana. She started the music. "Glue your eyes to me."

Amelia Bedelia was stunned. She had

followed the steps up to now, but putting glue in your eyes is a terrible idea. What grown-up would say that? She looked around. She was relieved to see that no one had any glue. Everyone was watching Dana very closely and doing just what she did.

Dana started them off just tapping their toes right-left right-left right-left right-left. Then they tapped their heels right-left eight times. That led into eight toe taps with each foot, then to eight brush-and-drags, then to eight more toe taps on each foot, then heels again, then toes again. Then they were back to where they started.

Smiles began appearing on the faces of the dancers. Amelia Bedelia was sure

that everyone was thinking just what she was thinking. She turned to her mom, who was tapping away next to her. "This is fun!" she said. "We sound amazing!"

When Dana finished the routine, everyone started clapping. Dana held up her hands and clapped right back at them. Then she leaned over to hear what a man in a coat and tie was saying to her. She smiled and picked up the bullhorn again.

"Bravo, Tepper Tappers! We just set a new state record: three hundred and forty-eight dancers were all tapping to the same tune!" Cheers and

applause broke out once more. Everyone started to tap and twirl and hug their neighbors. Amelia Bedelia's mother grabbed her hands and swung her around.

The man on the other side of Amelia Bedelia began dancing with a blond lady who was wearing a pink gown with fluffy feathers around the hem. His outfit was not so great. He carried a cane under his arm and wore a tall black hat that reminded Amelia Bedelia of the hats snowmen wore. He had on a stiff white shirt, black trousers, and a black jacket that was split up the back.

Amelia Bedelia gasped. "I'm sorry to tell you this," she said. "But your jacket is ripped in the back, right up the middle!"

The lady in the pink gown laughed,

and so did he. "Those are tails!" he said. "My jacket was designed like that on purpose. See how nicely my tails move when I dance?"

The man did a quick tap dance, twirling around so fast that his tails flew out to the sides.

"Wow!" said Amelia Bedelia. "That was amazing for someone who needs a cane!"

The man and his partner laughed even louder.

"I don't need a cane to dance," he said. "I make this cane dance, like so."

He repeated the dance steps, but this time he swung his cane in an arc through the air, striking the tip on the ground *click-click-click* as he tapped. He made his cane sound like a third foot tap dancing.

Amelia Bedelia was amazed. This dancer could actually tap his feet, spin, tap his cane, and dance with a partner, all at the same time! A crowd had gathered to watch them. Naturally, Wanda pushed through it. She grabbed Amelia Bedelia's mother by the arm and introduced both her and Amelia Bedelia to the wonderful dancers

as soon as the applause had died down.

"Georgie," said Wanda. "Show my sister-in-law a step or two." While Amelia Bedelia's mother was getting a lesson in tapping and twirling from the man in tails and his partner, Amelia Bedelia spotted Dana approaching. She had come down to the street to mingle with her record-breaking dancers.

"Wanda!" said Dana, hugging her. "Glad you made it!"

Wanda introduced Amelia Bedelia to Dana. "Wouldn't miss it," said Wanda, eyes sparkling. "Dana, this is my niece. Amelia Bedelia, meet Dana. You'll be seeing a lot more of each other." Then Wanda winked.

Dana smiled at Amelia Bedelia. Amelia

Bedelia smiled back, but she couldn't help wondering . . . how much more of Dana could there possibly be, and when would she be seeing it?

Just then Amelia Bedelia's mother came spinning to a stop. "Let's go shop the sale!" she said.

Chapter 3

Care to Dance?
NO!!!

When Amelia Bedelia, her mother, and Aunt Wanda got back home, they were so surprised, they almost called the police.

"What's that noise?" said Wanda, putting her ear to the door.

WHIRRRR-RRRRR-WWWRRRRR.

Amelia Bedelia's mother shook her head. "Sounds familiar," she said.

WHIRRRR-RRRR-WWWRRRRR

"Sounds like a vacuum cleaner," said Amelia Bedelia, stepping inside. She saw something she had never seen before. Her father was running their vacuum cleaner back and forth, sucking up the popcorn that had landed all over the family room.

"This is a proud moment," said Wanda.

"What?" bellowed Amelia Bedelia's

father. He turned off the vacuum cleaner and the room got quiet.

"I'm proud of you!" yelled Wanda, cupping her hands to her mouth.

"Thanks," said Amelia Bedelia's father. "So why are you yelling at me?"

Amelia Bedelia's mother put down the Tepper's shopping bags.

"Honey, what's this?" said Amelia Bedelia's father. "I clean up the family room and you clean out our bank account?"

"Oh, please. It's the annual sale," said Wanda. "Your wife saved tons of money."

"We didn't even use money," said Amelia Bedelia. "Mom used a little plastic card."

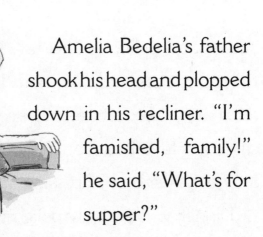

Amelia Bedelia's father shook his head and plopped down in his recliner. "I'm famished, family!" he said, "What's for supper?"

Amelia Bedelia's mother turned to Wanda and said, "I'd ask you to stay for dinner, but we're just having leftovers tonight."

"Oh, I adore leftovers," said Wanda. "The flavors get more intense. I'll whip up my anchovy-raspberry dressing for the salad."

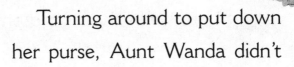

Turning around to put down her purse, Aunt Wanda didn't

see what Amelia Bedelia saw. Her father rolled his eyes and stuck out his tongue, and her mother arched her eyebrows and sighed. How bad could Aunt Wanda's anchovy-raspberry dressing be?

Dinner was actually delightful, and the salad was very tasty. Aunt Wanda told funny stories about Amelia Bedelia's father  when he was growing up. The stories reminded Amelia Bedelia that her dad had been young once, just like her.

After dessert, Wanda said, "Amelia Bedelia, now I can give you part two of your early birthday present. Are you ready?"

Amelia Bedelia clapped her hands as though she was still five years old. Aunt Wanda always gave her the best presents. She had a special talent for picking something fun and exciting and surprising. Amelia Bedelia couldn't expect a pony, but she'd never get matching socks and underwear, either.

"Here you go," said Wanda, handing an envelope to Amelia Bedelia.

Amelia Bedelia looked puzzled as she opened it and read the card.

"Dance lessons?" she asked.

"Dance lessons!" said Wanda. "Ten lessons at Dana's School of Dance."

"But . . ." This didn't seem like

the sort of present Wanda usually gave her.

"Honey," said Amelia Bedelia's mother. "What do you say?"

"But I was hoping for a drum set," said Amelia Bedelia.

"Drums?" said her father. "Why do you want drums?"

"Thank you, Wanda," said Amelia Bedelia's mother. "My daughter is being rude. Sweetie, tap dancing is like drumming, with your feet. Please thank your aunt."

"Oh, I'm sure it's going to be just ballet stuff," said Amelia Bedelia. "And I really don't want to be a ballerina!" She jumped out of her chair, twirled, and leaped around the table, waving her arms in wacky ways before slumping back into her seat.

"Bravo!" said her father, clapping his hands. "You could teach dance lessons."

Amelia Bedelia crossed her arms and glared at her father. She totally understood why Aunt Wanda thought her younger brother was a pest. Sometimes her dad made her crazy.

"You picked up tap dancing right away, Amelia Bedelia," said Wanda. "You're a natural. Just give dancing a chance."

"I don't understand you," said Amelia Bedelia's mother. "You usually love to try new things.

Plus, we had fun today with Dana. What would change your mind?"

Amelia Bedelia began drumming on the table.

"Forget drums," said her father. "You're dreaming, pumpkin."

"What if I get you a drum to dance with?" asked Aunt Wanda.

"Wanda!" said Amelia Bedelia's father. "Don't encourage her."

"Don't discourage her," said Wanda.

Amelia Bedelia's mother stood up. She could see a storm brewing. "I'll help you clear the table, Amelia Bedelia," she said.

"Okay, Mom," said Amelia Bedelia.

She cleared her aunt's plate. "Thanks for the dancing lessons, Aunt Wanda. I'll give them a try."

Wanda gave her a hug and said, "That's the spirit, honey."

"You don't have to get me a drum too," said Amelia Bedelia. "You're way too busy. Dad says you are a real busybody."

Wanda glared at her brother. "Do tell," she said.

"Amelia Bedelia," called her mother. "I need your help in the kitchen."

Amelia Bedelia's father turned red. "What I meant, Wanda, is that you always have a lot on your plate."

"No she doesn't," said Amelia Bedelia. "Look at her plate, Dad. It's clean and empty."

"Amelia Bedelia!" called her mother again. "Come in here *now!*"

the clean plate club!

Chapter 4

Say What Kind of Mall?

Amelia Bedelia's first dance lesson was the very next day. Her mother called the dance school to find out what Amelia Bedelia would need to wear. Then she raced around town buying everything, picked up Amelia Bedelia after school, and drove her to Dana's School of Dance.

Amelia Bedelia looked through the

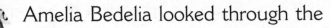

shopping bags in the car.

"What's this?" she asked, holding up a skimpy piece of fabric.

"It was on the list," said her mother.

Amelia Bedelia read the tag. "Leotard?" she asked.

"Check," said her mother.

"No, it's solid pink, not checked," said Amelia Bedelia. She held up another item. "Do I have to wear these?"

"Those are tights," said her mother.

"I need to move freely," said Amelia Bedelia. "Tights are tight. I need looses."

Amelia Bedelia's mother smiled. "I'll buy you a pair of looses as soon as someone invents them," she said. "The

school is in this mall." She
turned into a parking lot next
to a long one-story building.

"This is weird," said Amelia
Bedelia. "What kind of mall is this?"

"Strip," said her mother.

"No!" said Amelia Bedelia.
"I'm not taking my clothes off
in a mall parking lot."

"Of course not, sweetie," said
her mother. "I'm sure Dana has a
changing room. Come on, we're running
late."

They got out of the car and walked
toward a big window with decals of
ballerinas flitting around curly gold letters
that said DANA'S SCHOOL OF DANCE. To

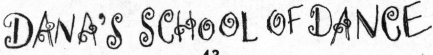

DANA'S SCHOOL OF DANCE

Amelia Bedelia, the sign might as well have said 10,000 POISONOUS SNAKES INSIDE. Her mother opened the door, took her by the hand, and practically had to drag her inside.

"Hello, hello! We met yesterday," Dana said. "I'm Dana."

"I'm still Amelia Bedelia," said Amelia Bedelia.

"We're late," said Amelia Bedelia's mother.

"No problem," said Dana. "Your daughter can change quickly in the girls' dressing room and meet the rest of the class in Studio One, through that door."

"Have fun, sweetie," said Amelia Bedelia's mother. "I'll be back in a bit."

Amelia Bedelia changed into her leotard and tights and entered Studio One. There were five other kids in the class. Most of them were smiling and looked happy to be there. One did not. The tallest kid was actually frowning, clutching a skateboard. He looked like Amelia Bedelia felt. She went over and stood next to him, even though he was a boy.

"Okay, everyone, this is Amelia Bedelia, and she is joining our class today," said Dana. "She is a talented tap dancer. She picks up things quickly."

"Hi, I'm Brad," said the boy. "Brad McDonald." His skateboard slipped out of his hand, onto the floor. Amelia Bedelia picked it up and gave it back to him.

"Thanks," said Brad. "You really *do* pick up things quickly."

"Over here is Gracie," said Dana. A girl curtsied—she had a skirt that floated around her like a pink cloud, and a matching pink leotard and tights. Amelia Bedelia looked down at her own outfit, which seemed loose and baggy compared to Gracie's. Now she wished her tights were tighter.

"Hi, I'm Willow," said a girl in a tie-dyed leotard, giving a quick little wave from across the room. Amelia Bedelia waved back. She liked Willow immediately.

"Last but not least," said Dana, "the Hernandez twins."

A boy and girl who didn't even look related did a quick, complicated dance step together. It ended with the boy twirling the girl around, then catching her as she fell back across his thigh.

"Wow!" said Amelia Bedelia.

Those kids were incredible dancers! Amelia Bedelia felt like running right out of Studio One and racing home to play with Finally in the yard. Luckily, she had a strategy for this type of situation. Whenever she didn't know what to do, she asked a question. Besides, she was curious. "How can you be twins?" she asked. "You don't even look alike."

"We're fraternal twins," said the boy. "I'm Alex."

"I'm Alexandra," said the girl. "Our mom named us so that when she hollers 'Alex,' at least one of us answers."

"Smart mom," said Dana. "As you can tell, Amelia Bedelia, the students in this class have a wide variety of experience. Don't worry. You'll catch up. And you'll have fun, I promise. Now, let's get some basic moves under your belt."

Amelia Bedelia looked down at her

waist and panicked. She had no belt! Where would she put the basic moves? She looked around the studio quickly. None of the other kids wore belts either. Whew! She relaxed.

"Each week I'll bring in expert dancers to share their skills. My focus is modern dance. So let's start with some warm-up exercises while we think about how and why we move."

Dana asked Brad and Willow to drag a giant floor fan into the middle of the studio. She turned it on to the highest speed.

"Line up behind me," said Dana. "Put your arms in the air like this, and keep them loose. When you pass in front of the fan, imagine that you are tall grass in a storm."

Amelia Bedelia did not have to imagine too hard. The blast of air nearly knocked her over. She swayed back and forth with her arms in the air.

"Wonderful work!" said Dana. "Now. Again! Only this time, imagine you are a tree."

They all walked around again, this time pretending to be trees. Amelia Bedelia noticed that Willow had a huge smile on her face and she was moving her arms as if they were willow tree branches swaying in the wind.

Next they imagined they were waves at the beach, then eagles, then snakes. *Oh, well,* thought Amelia Bedelia, wiggling across the floor. At least there were not ten thousand poisonous snakes. She had to admit that she had more of a feeling for nature than she'd had before Dana's class.

Chapter 5

You Say Flamenco, I Say Flamingo

The next week when Amelia Bedelia arrived at Dana's, it looked as though Studio One was being remodeled. She almost crashed into Brad and Alex, who were carrying a big sheet of plywood.

"Watch it, watch it!" shouted Alex.

Amelia Bedelia jumped out of their way. Brad and Alex placed the plywood on the floor, right next to another sheet of plywood that they had already positioned. Amelia Bedelia watched the piece of plywood like a hawk. It did not do a thing. It just lay there on the floor.

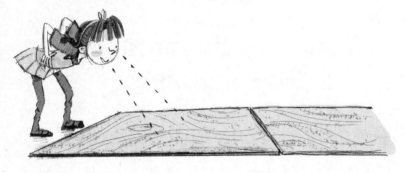

She wasn't sure what she had expected, but this was super boring.

"I think two sheets will be enough," said Dana. "Thanks, guys!" Now Amelia Bedelia was completely confused.

"You're putting sheets on the boards?" asked Amelia Bedelia. "Who would want

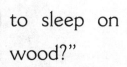

to sleep on wood?"

Dana laughed. She stepped on one board and then the other, bouncing lightly to make sure they were stable. "These are sheets of plywood, to protect my floor from our guest dancers today."

"They must be huge! How can dancers hurt a floor?" asked Amelia Bedelia. "How heavy are they?"

"Oh, they're light on their feet," said Dana. "But they hit the ground very hard with their heels."

"Harder than tap dancing?" asked Amelia Bedelia.

55

"Much harder," said Dana. "These are flamenco dancers."

"Hah!" said Brad. "This isn't dance class, this is a nature course! First we get to be grass blowing in the wind, and now we get to watch dancing birds."

"Birds? Dancing?" said Dana. "What are you talking about?" She gave Brad a bewildered look.

"You know, those goofy-looking pink birds with the big black beaks? The ones that stand on one leg?" he said.

"People stick plastic ones on their lawns. My sister

flamingo birds

loves those things, I think because—"

Dana exploded with laughter. The Hernandez twins were laughing so hard they could barely speak.

Brad just stood there, looking very confused. "What . . ."

Dana put her arm around Brad. "Oh, honey," she said, "the bird you're describing is a fla*mingo*. This is a dance called the fla*menco*, with a C instead of a G."

Just then, a couple came through the door of the studio. The man was carrying a guitar and the woman wore a lacy red shawl over a long black dress that was full and frilly at the bottom.

flamenco dancers →

57

"Everyone, this is Senor and Senora España," said Dana. "Pull up a piece of floor and sit down."

Amelia Bedelia, Alex, Alexandra, Willow, Brad, and Gracie sat in a circle around the plywood and listened.

"Flamenco comes from the south of Spain," said Senor España. "It combines music and song and dance to produce rhythmic patterns with percussion."

When Amelia Bedelia heard the word "percussion," she could not contain herself. She put her hand in the air. "But don't you need a drum for that?" she asked.

"There are other ways to play percussion," said Senor España, smiling. He strummed on his guitar and then

rapped on its shiny wooden surface with his knuckles. "Like that," he said.

"And like this," said Senora España. She raised her arms above her head and clapped out the same sequence of beats with her hands. "From the top to the bottom," she said. Then she produced the same pattern by striking her heels on the plywood floor.

Senor España played his guitar. "The best way to show you how it all works together is with a dance," he said. He began playing a beautiful melody, and his wife began clapping her hands and striking her heels very hard on the floor

at the same time. Gracie covered her ears. Amelia Bedelia loved it. She felt like she was sitting inside a giant popcorn popper.

When the dance was done, everyone clapped and then laughed, because it sounded like the dance was still going on. They could hear the echo of the percussion in their ears.

Pop! Pop! Po

The Españas began dancing again, much slower this time. Senora España held up her hands and demonstrated her claps in slow motion. The class joined in. As they got used to the rhythm, the guitar

and the dancing got faster, and soon their clapping sounded like applause. Suddenly, the Españas stopped playing and dancing and froze, but the class kept clapping. They both bowed and said, "Thank you, thank you!" Everyone laughed.

Senora España took Willow, Gracie,

Alexandra, and Amelia Bedelia to one side of the plywood floor to teach them some flamenco steps. Senora España actually had nails driven into the bottom of her shoes, but the girls put on their tap-dancing shoes, and they still managed to make a lot of noise!

Senor España gave Brad and Alex a short lesson on flamenco guitar techniques and beats.

There was time for one more dance. This time, Senor España played the guitar and danced as well. First Senora España would tap out a rhythm, then he would dance an answer to it, with the guitar uniting the two sequences of sound. Senora España unfurled a fan and used it to draw attention to the movement of her hand.

As Amelia sat there watching the Españas dance, she thought about the fact that flamenco was amazing but hot. If she had that fan, she would use it to cool herself off. She leaned over to Brad. "What are you thinking?" she whispered.

Brad was quiet for a moment. Then he whispered, "I think my sister is right. They would look great on our lawn."

Amelia Bedelia covered her mouth to keep from laughing out loud.

Chapter 6

The Best Teacher, Barre None

The next week, Amelia Bedelia was dreading the lesson as much as Gracie was looking forward to it. It was going to be all about ballet. Dana had invited her own ballet teacher to visit the class.

"It's okay," said Dana, talking on the phone as she walked into Studio One. "Take your time, drive safely." She

turned to the class. "Apparently there's a traffic jam, so Madame Dansova will be late. Let's warm up until she gets here. Spread out and find a spot near the mirror."

Amelia Bedelia found a spot near the back of the room. She was warm already, probably too warm for a place near the mirror.

"You call her Madame Dansova. Is she French?" asked Willow.

"No," said Dana. "She's Russian."

"But you told her not to hurry," said Amelia Bedelia.

"She is Russian because she's from Russia," said Dana.

"No wonder she's late," said Amelia

Bedelia. "Russia is really far away from here."

"Oh, she lives in this country now," said Dana. "And she'll be here any minute."

"Is she half French?" asked Willow. "My mom is."

"No, Madame Dansova is completely Russian," said Dana.

"We can wait," said Amelia Bedelia.

Dana looked puzzled. "Thank you, Amelia Bedelia," she said. "Now, did you know that many of the terms we use to describe steps in ballet are French?"

"Why French?" asked Alexandra.

Gracie raised her hand.

"Gracie?" said Dana.

Louis XIV

"King Louis XIV of France loved ballet so much that he started the first ballet school," said Gracie. "Since many of the steps were created at that school, they have French names."

"Thank you, Gracie," said Dana. "Madame Dansova was a ballet mistress at a very famous ballet company. We're lucky to have her."

"What does a ballet company make?" asked Brad. "Tutus?"

Everyone except Gracie and Dana began to laugh.

"DANCERS!"

They all turned to the doorway. The laughter ceased.

"Madame Dansova," said Dana, rushing to the door. "How wonderful to see you!" The ballet mistress wore a fur hat and muffler, even though it was fairly warm outside.

"A great ballet company makes one thing only," said Madame Dansova. "It makes great dancers. Dancers who move with such grace and style that you cannot take your eyes off them. You *must* watch them. They transport you to another world." She spoke precisely, with a thick Russian accent.

Amelia Bedelia glanced at Gracie. She seemed to be in a trance, in that other world completely, just from listening to Madame Dansova speak. The spell was broken when

Madame Dansova said, "All right, boys and girls, let's all go to the barre."

"I'm too young to go to a bar," said Brad.

salad bar

Everyone except Amelia Bedelia giggled. She had been thinking the same thing, but not as a joke.

"Not that kind of bar," said Dana. "And not a salad bar, or an all-you-can-eat taco bar. This one is spelled B-A-R-R-E, and it is right here," she said, patting the two long wooden handrails mounted one above the other along the sides of the room.

"We have one of those at home," said Alexandra. "We call it a banister."

taco bar

"Yup, that's what it looks like," said Alex.

"I like that," said Madame Dansova. "It

ballet barre

will help you scale the heights of ballet. Now turn to the side and hold the barre lightly with your left hand."

The class lined up and grabbed the barre. Dana moved to the other side of the

room, where they could all see her, and positioned herself at the barre there.

"Listen to Madame," she said, "and watch what I do."

"Heels together," said Madame Dansova. "Now turn your legs out, out, out until a big piece of pizza pie would fit between your feet."

They all understood. Except Brad.

"Your feet are much too far apart," said Madame to Brad.

"I love pizza," said Brad. "That's how much I would eat." But he understood now and scooted his feet closer together.

"Lovely, boys and girls!" said Madame Dansova. "Next, the demi-plié."

demi-plié

72

"That means 'half bend' in French," said Gracie.

Madame described the move and gave tips as Dana demonstrated it. "Heels together, feet on the floor. Now watch the diamond shape form between her legs as she bends."

The class did twenty demi-pliés with Dana while Madame strolled around the studio, correcting them one by one.

"Now time for a grand plié!" said Madame.

"Grand is French for—" Gracie started to say.

"We can guess," interrupted Alexandra.

Once again, Dana demonstrated the

step while Madame described the technique. "Start with a demi-plié, now bend deeper, let your heels come off the floor, deeper, knees out, back straight, deeper . . . deeper . . ."

The deeper they bent, the more they started to tip and teeter. No one wanted to admit that it was hard. But it was ridiculous! Everyone started to laugh, and then Willow lost her balance, falling backward on Alex, who fell on Alexandra, who took out the rest of the class in a giggling heap. Gracie was the only one left standing, because she had been in front of Willow. She ignored the mayhem and kept doing grand pliés.

"Brava!" said Madame. She led Gracie across the studio to Dana. "Help her with

her hands while I concentrate on these falling dominoes," she said.

After the class got untangled, Madame had them face the barre and hang on with both hands.

"And one, two, three, four, five." Madame counted and clapped and slinked around the studio like a tigress, as they did five more sets of ten grand pliés. Amelia Bedelia had never been so tired in her life!

"This is great," said Brad. "I use the same leg muscles skateboarding."

"Yes!" said Madame, smiling. "Ballet is a necessity of life! When I come back to Dana's studio, I will show you the five basic positions of ballet."

"But next week, everyone," said Dana, handing Madame her fur hat, "I

76

have something very different planned. You'll see!"

Amelia Bedelia was completely worn out when she got home. But she'd liked ballet more than she'd expected to, and she was curious about those five basic positions. What would they look like? Would they be easy or hard? In the meantime, she created the sixth position of ballet. She fell asleep, sprawled out on her father's recliner.

Chapter 7

Breaking into Dancing

A surprise thunderstorm made Amelia Bedelia and her mother late for the next dance class. When they arrived, they found Brad, Alex, Alexandra, Gracie, and Willow standing in front of the school with their parents or babysitters.

"The door is locked," said Gracie. "Where is Dana?"

"I don't know, sweetheart," said Amelia Bedelia's mother. "Dana should be here."

Three other people were standing near the dance school too. They all wore the same thing—basketball jerseys from different teams, long shorts and sneakers, and plain black baseball caps. The tallest one approached and asked, "Is Dana coming?"

"We don't know," said Amelia Bedelia's mother. "May I help you?"

"My name is Bill," he said. "Dana asked us to come and give a demonstration today."

"Oh, there must be some mistake," said Gracie's mother politely. "This isn't a basketball clinic. It's a dance class."

Bill smiled. The other two laughed.

"We aren't basketball players," said one of them.

"We're dancers," said the other.

"Dancers?" said Amelia Bedelia.

"Break dancers," said Bill.

"Cool," said Brad. "Remember, you guys? Dana said our next class was going to be totally different!"

Amelia Bedelia was excited. She could tell that the others were excited too. She had seen break dancing on television, but it would be really great to learn how to do it herself.

Just then, Wanda drove up and stopped outside the school.

"I've got the keys, everyone!" she called, getting out of her car. "We're all set for class." She opened the door to the dance school and let the students in. Then she turned to Amelia Bedelia's mother and took her aside. "I'm glad you're here. Any chance you can stick around until class is over?"

"Where's Dana?" asked Amelia Bedelia's mother.

"At the emergency room," said Wanda. "Her back steps were wet from the rain. She slipped and—"

"Oh my goodness," said Amelia Bedelia's mother, bringing her hands up to her mouth. "Of course!"

"Let those break dancers run the class," said Wanda. "Bill is fabulous. I've got to bring Dana some things from home. I'll come by your house with a full report later."

The class gathered in Studio One, in a semicircle around the break dancers, who were stretching and spinning to the music.

"Are you guys doing warm-ups or actual dance moves?" asked Alex.

"Doesn't matter," said Bill. "As long as it gets the job done."

Bill and the other dancers, whose names were Rita and Jasper, were amazing. They kept trying to outdo one another, spinning on their heads and on just one hand, moving this way and that, trying out sequences with incredible super-fast footwork. Jasper launched himself into the air, landed in a handstand, and froze in that position.

When the music stopped, the dancers helped the class master an easy six-step, a basic first move in break dancing. It was way harder than the dancers made it look, even in slow motion. Amelia Bedelia got tangled up with Willow. Gracie

Imagine a big circle in front of you.

tripped over Alex, and Brad and Alexandra ended up in a heap on the floor, laughing hysterically.

① Step out with your left foot.

② Cross behind with your right foot.

③ Left foot uncrosses.

④ Cross with your right foot.

⑤ Step back with your left foot.

⑥ Step back to starting.

"Too bad Dana missed break dancing," said Amelia Bedelia to her mom as they drove home. "I bet she would have loved it!"

"Oh, honey, I know! I just hope Dana's all right!" said her mother.

"Oh no! While we were break dancing, do you think she really broke something?" asked Amelia Bedelia. Tears welled up in her eyes.

Amelia Bedelia's mother turned in to the driveway. "Aunt Wanda is right behind us," she said. "We'll get a report."

Amelia Bedelia's father was home

OUCH!

already, so they all sat in the kitchen while Wanda gave them the bad news.

"When Dana slipped, she broke her leg in two places," she said.

"I thought she fell on the steps," said Amelia Bedelia. "Did she fall somewhere else too?"

"Dana didn't fall in two different places," said her mother.

"The bone in her leg is broken in two places," her father explained.

"That's horrible!" said Amelia Bedelia. "Can we visit her?"

"That would be nice, sweetie," said Wanda, "but Dana needs to rest."

"No more dance class, I guess," said Amelia Bedelia.

"Actually," said Wanda, "Dana made me promise to keep the class going with demonstrations like the one you had today. I'll arrange for the dancers until Dana can get back on her feet."

Amelia Bedelia hugged Aunt Wanda. "I know! You can show us how to tap dance!" she said.

"Your aunt Wanda has been tap dancing her whole life," said Amelia Bedelia's father. "She's an expert by now!"

Chapter 8

Ballet —— What's the Pointe?

When Madame Dansova got wind of Dana's accident, she returned right away to teach another ballet class. As it turned out, Amelia Bedelia's biggest worry was not getting her body into the five basic positions of ballet. It was keeping her hair in one place.

While the class was

warming up, Madame said, "Miss Bedelia, your hair keeps flippy-flopping in your face. You must wear it like I do, in a bun." Madame pointed to the round, hairy knob on the back of her head.

Amelia Bedelia wondered what kind of bun Madame Dansova kept under her hair. Sourdough? Whole wheat? Burger?

Before she could ask, though,
Madame clapped her hands,
and class began.

"We will start by learning the first position," said Madame. "And in the spirit of first things first, remember that the best dancers dance with their ears."

Amelia Bedelia had heard of people playing by ear, but dancing by ear sounded super painful.

"Listen closely, boys and girls," continued Madame, "and you will get off on the right foot."

She demonstrated the correct arm position, saying, "Hold your arms out in front of you, gently. Pretend you carry a fragile bubble of soap. Now, turn your legs

out, from your hips down to your heels."

"Heels together, Miss Bedelia," said Madame. "Look at Gracie, and put your best foot forward."

Amelia Bedelia slid her left foot out ahead of her right foot.

"Miss Bedelia! What are you doing?" asked Madame. "Why do you put your left foot in front?"

"I like my left foot better than my right," said Amelia Bedelia.

"You have a favorite foot?" asked Madame.

"I'm right-handed," said Amelia Bedelia. "So I am left-footed. I like to make things balance."

"Yes! Balance is very important," said Madame, "but you are getting off on the wrong foot, Miss Bedelia."

Amelia Bedelia switched her feet and put the right foot forward and the left one back. "Is this better?" she asked, looking down at her feet. "Now I'll get off on my right foot." Amelia Bedelia's hair fell in her face. Madame was not pleased.

"Miss Gracie," said Madame. "Your first position is perfect. Please escort Miss Bedelia to the dressing room and show her how to fix her hair for the ballet so she can see what she is doing. Seeing is just as important as listening."

"Yes, Madame," said Gracie.

Amelia Bedelia and Gracie headed to the changing room. When they got there, Gracie removed a handful of hairpins from the back of her head and then, reaching up, she pulled a black stretchy out of her hair. Amelia Bedelia was shocked.

"Gracie," she said, "your hair is just as short as my hair."

"Yup," said Gracie.

Amelia Bedelia got a notebook out of

her backpack. "What's your secret recipe for a ballet bun?" she asked.

Gracie giggled. Then she grabbed a brush and got to work on Amelia Bedelia's hair, explaining what she was doing as she brushed and twisted and pinned. Amelia Bedelia wrote down directions and drew little sketches as Gracie worked.

"Ta-dah!" said Gracie as they looked in the mirror together.

How to bake a BALLET BUN:

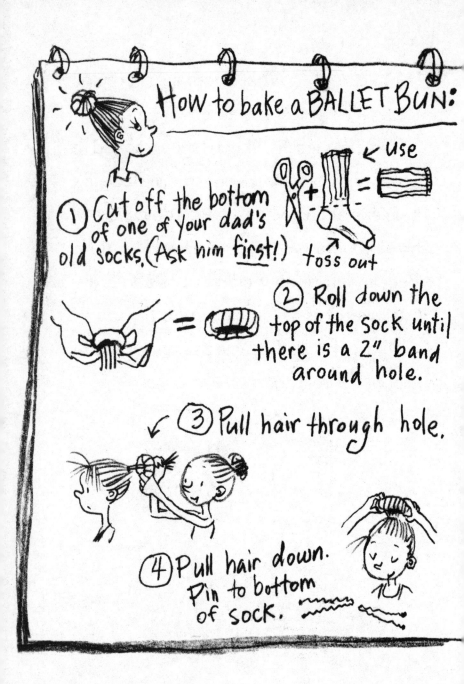

← use

① Cut off the bottom of one of your dad's old socks. (Ask him **first**!) *toss out*

② Roll down the top of the sock until there is a 2" band around hole.

③ Pull hair through hole.

④ Pull hair down. Pin to bottom of sock.

"Wow," said Amelia Bedelia. "Thanks, Gracie!"

Gracie used a spare sock and put her hair in a new bun too, and they rejoined the class.

BRAVA!

"Brava, Miss Bedelia!" said Madame. "Now that your hair looks the part, you'll soon be on your toes like Gracie." Gracie stood up on the very tips of her toes.

"I get the point, Madame," said Amelia Bedelia. "Finally!"

Chapter 9

Salsa Inside and Out

If Wanda's body was busy before Dana broke her leg, it was even busier now. She came to the next class out of breath, carrying grocery bags.

"Whew!" she said. "I've been all over the place, making calls and running errands. I didn't have time for lunch. Let's start off with some salsa."

"Yes!" said Alex.

"That's our favorite dance," said Alexandra, clapping. The twins could not contain themselves. Alex turned on the music. Within seconds, Alex and Alexandra were dancing, back and forth, back and forth.

"We learned when we were little, from watching our mom and dad," said Alex. "They taught us this new step just last week." Alexandra whirled away

from Alex, then he twirled her back while switching hands at the same time. Everyone clapped.

"That looks fun," said Willow. "Can you show us how to dance like that?"

The twins took turns showing the class the basic salsa step. They walked forward while counting one, two, three, and backward while counting five, six, seven. "Your feet don't move on four or eight," said Alex. "So we don't really count them."

· Steps to DANcE Salsa ·

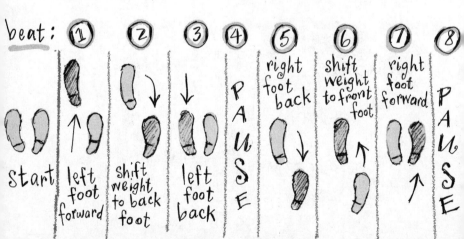

beat: ① ② ③ ④ ⑤ ⑥ ⑦ ⑧

start | left foot forward | shift weight to back foot | left foot back | PAUSE | right foot back | shift weight to front foot | right foot forward | PAUSE

"It's more like a pause," said Alexandra. "You can count in your head, if you want."

"Eight steps?" said Wanda. "My salsa takes three easy steps."

"Three steps?" said Alex.

"Cool!" said Alexandra. "Show us!"

Wanda reached into her grocery bag, pulled out a big jar of salsa, and said, "Step one, open the jar. Step two, pour salsa into a bowl. Step three, open bag of chips."

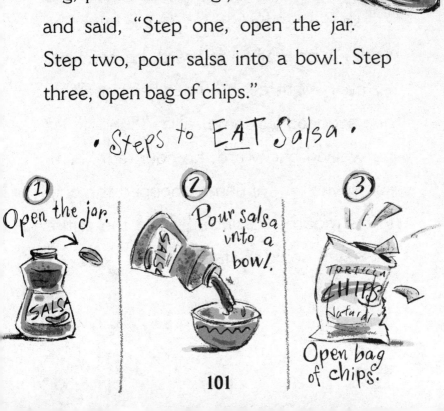

• Steps to EAT Salsa •

① Open the jar.

② Pour salsa into a bowl!

③ Open bag of chips.

Wanda grabbed a chip, scooped up some salsa, and said, "I was so busy that I missed lunch today. Dig in!"

"Thanks, Aunt Wanda!" said Amelia Bedelia, helping herself to the surprise treat. The other dancers dug in too.

Alex grabbed Amelia Bedelia's hand. "I'll show you the famous double salsa," he said. As he walked forward, he counted, "One, two, three . . ." Then he took a chip and scooped up some salsa. "Scoop!" As he walked backward, he counted, "Five, six, seven . . ." Then he popped the chip in his mouth. "*Crunch!*" Soon the entire class was doing the famous double salsa.

"Hey," said Amelia Bedelia, crunching a chip. "I'm doing salsa inside and out."

Wanda laughed loudest of all, until she noticed that an elderly couple had stopped outside on the sidewalk. They were staring in the window, with their hands cupped on the glass, around their faces. No one knew how long they had been standing there.

"Gosh," said Wanda. "I hope we weren't too loud."

"Are anyone's grandparents coming today?" asked Willow.

Everyone shook their heads no.

"Were the kids making too much noise?" asked Wanda, opening the door and poking her head out.

"Not at all," said the woman.

"We thoroughly enjoyed it," said the man. "My name is Bob Quinn, and this is my wife, Lois."

"Before we retired," explained Lois, "we ran a school for ballroom dancing, so we love seeing these kids dance."

"Brings back lots of memories for us," said Bob.

"Come inside, come inside," said

Wanda as she held the door open for them. "Meet the kids and try some salsa—eating or dancing."

"We taught lots of folks how to dance in our day," said Lois.

"Is there any chance you'd give us a demonstration?" asked Wanda.

"We'd love to do that," said Bob. "Honey, let's rumba!"

Bob and Lois walked slowly, like Amelia Bedelia's grandparents. But once they joined hands and began to dance, they were graceful and fast. They glided over the floor, matching each other step for step, turn for turn. Whenever Bob twirled Lois away under his arm, she would come spinning back again—

HONK-HONK HONNNKKKK!!!!

Bob yanked Lois up. "That's our bus! We're late!" he said.

HONK-HONK!

The spell cast by the Quinns' dancing was shattered, and Wanda sprang into action. She stalked out of the studio and approached the bus parked right outside.

"Hey, lady!" yelled the driver. "Have you seen an older couple—"

HoNk-HoNkHoooOONN𝘒𝘒!!!

"Keep your shirt on, pal," said Wanda. "They'll be out in a minute."

Amelia Bedelia could see that driver was wearing a jacket as well as a shirt, and from the look on his face, he wasn't her Aunt Wanda's pal.

"Here comes trouble," she said to Gracie.

"You know," said Bob, "we'd love to visit again. Just let us know when your next show is. We'll bring a busload of

521 million years old

fossils just like us to watch you perform."

When Wanda came back from helping the Quinns onto the bus, Amelia Bedelia noticed that she had a faraway look in her eyes. The few times Amelia Bedelia had seen that look before, life had gotten a bit crazier.

"Hmm . . . Why not?" said Wanda under her breath.

"I love fossils!" said Amelia Bedelia to Gracie.

Chapter 10

Difference Makes All the Difference

Amelia Bedelia got a ride home from Aunt Wanda that day. It gave them a chance to talk.

"I like dance class way more than I thought I would," said Amelia Bedelia. "Thanks for the present."

Aunt Wanda smiled. "I'm happy to hear that," she said. "I was afraid you

really wouldn't enjoy it at all!"

"I like the other kids a lot," said Amelia Bedelia. "They are so different from my friends at school and from each other."

"I'm glad you like that difference," said Aunt Wanda. "That's very grown-up."

"Sure, Aunt Wanda," said Amelia Bedelia. "Differences make things different. It would be boring if everyone was the same."

"That's very true," said Aunt Wanda. They rode along in silence for a few blocks until Aunt Wanda said, "I've been thinking. Wouldn't it be nice to have a recital?"

"A recital?" said Amelia Bedelia. "You mean reciting poems and stories and stuff?"

"No, not words. Dances," said Aunt Wanda. "In a dance recital, dancers perform dances they've learned and show their family and friends what they've been doing in class."

"Great," said Amelia Bedelia. "That sounds really fun."

"You could help me by being a choreographer— that's what we call someone who

111

plans a dance," said Aunt Wanda. "The best dances tell a story to share an idea or emotion."

"Okay," said Amelia Bedelia. "I'd probably be good at that. Did you know that Willow is a really good artist? And Brad skateboards. Gracie is also great at gymnastics. Alex and Alexandra can do almost any dance. Kids should do what comes naturally."

Chapter 11

"Do It for Dana!"

Amelia Bedelia's entire dance class loved the idea of a dance recital.

"We'll do it for Dana!" said Willow.

Those words, "Do It for Dana," became their motto, keeping them planning, creating, and rehearsing even when they were tired and out of ideas.

They had just begun figuring out what

dances to include in the recital when a new group of dancers walked into the studio.

"Aloha," said a man wearing a shirt that also said ALOHA. "We're from the Polynesian Society at the college. You booked us to teach the hula to your dance students."

"Oh, aloha! Welcome!" said Wanda. "We've been focusing on our recital, so we're buzzing around like bees. Alexandra, take our guests to the dressing room so they can change while I set things up."

All of a sudden, *another* group of dancers walked

into the studio. They were all wearing kilts.

"Hi there, you must be Dana," said a woman carrying a fiddle. "We're from the Celtic Club."

Alex nodded toward one of the boys, nudged Brad, and whispered, "Nice skirt."

"Not as nice as mine," said Brad. "I'm from the McDonald clan, and my tartan is *awesome*."

"I'm so glad you could make it," said Wanda. She was definitely going with the flow. Dana must have invited the Celtic Club before she broke her leg.

This was going to be an interesting class!

At that moment the Polynesian Society dancers returned to the studio. They were all barefoot and wearing leis and grass skirts, even the boys.

Alex and Brad just looked at each other and laughed.

Amelia Bedelia, Gracie, Willow, Alex, Brad, and Alexandra sat on the floor in Studio One. The Polynesians danced first,

moving two steps to the left, then two steps to the right, with flowing hand movements that told a story about fish swimming in the ocean, fisherman pulling them ashore in nets, and then everyone having a feast.

Then the dancers from the Celtic Club demonstrated the difference between a Highland fling and Irish step dancing. Everyone watched the dancers step over and between a sword and scabbard in the Scottish sword dance. The dancers kept their arms by their sides or overhead, but their footwork was incredibly complex.

"Amazing," said Wanda. "This was a happy accident. It's so interesting to watch these different dance styles from opposite sides of the world side by side."

"Yeah," said Gracie. "The Polynesian dancers have simple footwork but very complicated hand gestures."

"And the Celtic dancers are stiff from

the waist up," said Willow, "but they express themselves through their feet."

"They have one thing in common, though," said Alex. "All the guys wear skirts!"

One of the Polynesian dancers pulled Alex into their group, put a grass skirt on him, then showed him how to sway his hips and tell a story with his hands. Alexandra could not stop laughing at the sight of her brother doing the hula. Then the whole class got a chance to practice with both troupes. Toward the end of the class, the Celtic dancers taught the hula dancers their steps, and the hula dancers taught the Celtic dancers how to sway and move their hands.

Everyone was laughing and learning new things. Amelia Bedelia was working on her Scottish footwork when she bumped into Aunt Wanda, who was doing the hula.

"I wish the whole world could be like this every day," Amelia Bedelia said.

"This is a start," said Wanda.

Chapter 12

Birds of a Feather
Dance Together

On the Saturday of the recital, Amelia Bedelia's father dropped her off at Dana's School of Dance early. She had misplaced the sock Gracie had given her for her bun, so she had grabbed a single sock from the laundry room.

"Hold it. Where did you find my sock?" her dad said as she was getting out of the car.

"It was in the laundry room, where Mom keeps all the lost socks," said Amelia Bedelia.

"Well, the other one is in my sock drawer," said her father. "Thanks for finding it, honey. It's my favorite!"

Amelia Bedelia's father grabbed his sock, gave Amelia Bedelia a quick kiss, and drove off.

Amelia Bedelia was happy to help, but now she had no way to put up her hair. She couldn't ask Gracie for another sock. That would be embarrassing. How could she make her bun? She searched through her backpack and discovered the perfect thing. It was a bagel she had forgotten to

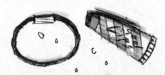

122

eat. She used her finger to enlarge the hole in the center, pushed her hair through it, and used bobby pins to secure the ends.

"Perfect," said Amelia Bedelia. "No one would guess that my bun is a bagel."

Aunt Wanda and the dancers set up chairs around the edge of Studio One. The audience grew quickly. Bob and Lois Quinn and their friends arrived on a bus. A few minutes after they came in, the bus driver walked in too. Dana zoomed in on her own chair—a wheelchair. She had her leg propped up in a cast. She parked next to Madame Dansova. The Españas came and the break dancers came and so did the Celtic Club and Polynesian Society troupes. And of course, there were parents, grandparents, and brothers and sisters and babysitters. Finally it was time for the recital to begin.

"Thank you for coming out to support our kids," said Wanda. "They have done a terrific job, learning all sorts of dances from various countries and cultures. They put this show together in honor of their teacher, Dana."

Everyone clapped as Dana spun her wheelchair around. "I would tell them to break a leg, but I beat them to it!" she said, smiling.

"Break a leg?" whispered Amelia Bedelia to Brad. He lifted his eyebrows and shrugged his shoulders. But then the audience laughed, so Amelia Bedelia decided it must be okay.

Willow danced the first dance. She had hung up a roll of paper as tall as she was and put pots of paint and paintbrushes on the floor beneath it. The music started, and so did Willow. As a jazz saxophone solo played, Willow began a modern dance. Moving back and forth in front of the paper, she picked up brushes, dabbing paint here and there. When the music finished, so had she.

"Hey," said Bill. "I can see a

guy playing a saxophone!" Sure enough, Willow had managed to paint an abstract portrait of a saxophonist. The applause grew louder and Willow bowed deeply.

Brad then put on hip-hop music and danced some break-dance moves that he had adapted to his skateboard routine. He spun, leaped, zoomed, and rolled around the studio. His dance earned some *oooohs* and *ahhhhs* and lots of applause from the audience. While he bowed, hip-hop was replaced by Hawaiian music, and Amelia Bedelia, Alexandra, Gracie, and Willow entered the studio. They swayed from side to side, waving long pieces of blue fabric along the floor. It looked just like the ocean.

Alex appeared, wearing a grass skirt. He set up a big cardboard palm tree that had been painted brown and green. Then he leaned against it, strumming a ukulele. When he put his hand to his brow to look out over the waves, the music changed to Scottish bagpipes and Brad returned, skateboarding between the waves. It looked

exactly as though he was surfing, except that he wore a kilt and not a wetsuit. When Brad landed on the island, the music changed back to a Hawaiian melody. The girls danced off the stage while Alex showed Brad how to hula.

In the audience, Amelia Bedelia's father took off his glasses and rubbed his eyes. "Did I just see a Scotsman surf to Hawaii and learn how to hula?"

he whispered to Amelia Bedelia's mother.

"With dance anything is possible," dear, " she said, patting his arm.

The music changed back to bagpipes again, and now Brad taught Alex the Highland fling. They leaped over his skateboard, jumping back and forth with their hands in the air as though they were doing a sword dance. Then they both stood on the skateboard and whizzed off the stage together, Alex carrying the

palm tree under his arm.

Their dance had given the girls a chance to change costumes for their performance. The long pieces of blue cloth still on stage were perfect for what was about to happen.

Wanda stood up and moved to the center of the studio. "The class dedicates this next dance to their ballet teacher, Madame Dansova," she said, nodding to the applauding audience. "The students wanted to perform a pas de deux, which means a dance with two people. However, they had trouble reading the

French term. Our choreographer thought it was 'pass the ducks,' and so we like to think of this dance as 'The Ugly Duckling Meets Swan Lake.'"

Amelia Bedelia and Willow entered the studio first. They wore leotards with cardboard cutouts attached on either side. They each looked like a bright yellow rubber ducky bathtub toy. Swimming side by side, they were very wide. Behind them came Alexandra

BRAVO! —BRAVO!

wearing a costume that . . . well, looked ugly. She kept trying to paddle past the two rubber ducks, but they wouldn't let her. Finally she swam around them, heading toward the back wall. The duckies were so wide that the audience lost sight of her.

When the two duckies parted, Alexandra had disappeared. Gracie, dressed as a gorgeous swan, had taken her place. The duckies dipped their heads as the swan passed between them. She was dancing on her tiptoes, en pointe. Gracie smiled and fluttered her white, feathery wings. The audience applauded and did not stop. Madame, who had started to laugh when Amelia Bedelia and Willow first appeared, had not stopped laughing the whole time. She stood and clapped the loudest. "Brava!" she yelled. "Brava!"

As the four girls took their curtain call, Amelia Bedelia, hampered by the cardboard ducky costume, bent too far forward. The bagel that had given shape to her bun rolled across the stage.

Brava! Brava! BRAVA!

"A bagel?" said Madame Dansova.
"I said a *bun*, Miss Bedelia!"

Amelia Bedelia was glad that her hair was flopping in her face. It covered her blushing, bright red cheeks.

Chapter 13

And Now, from a Lawn near You . . .

After intermission, the audience returned for one final dance. There was now a patch of fake grass in the middle of the studio. Two pink plastic flamingoes stood on it. The audience, though, was focused on another pair—Alex and Alexandra. They were each standing on one leg, and they were dressed in pink leotards, with big black beaks strapped over their noses. Alex started strumming on his guitar. Suddenly, their feet came down hard at the same time.

The twins launched into an incredible flamenco routine. Their feet seemed to talk to each other and to the guitar. At one point, Alexandra spread her wings like huge pink fans, just the way Senora España had spread her shawl. Maybe they had

practiced a lot, or maybe it was because they were twins and thought alike, but Alex and Alexandra performed flawlessly.

When they finished, everyone jumped up, applauding wildly and calling out, "Bravo! Brava! Olé, Pink Flamencos!"

Bravo! Brava! Olé!

Amelia Bedelia's mother had brought two bouquets of flowers from her garden. The class presented them to Wanda and Dana. They both bowed, then tossed the bouquets into the air so that flowers rained down on the dancers.

Then Wanda pushed Dana's chair, and a conga line formed behind her. Soon absolutely everyone was dancing. Amelia Bedelia grabbed the conga drum that Dana kept in the corner of the studio and

began broadcasting the beat. Dancing and drumming with family and friends— this was Amelia Bedelia's idea of heaven.

Chapter 14

Wanda Around

"Let's take it to the streets!" hollered Wanda. She held open the door to Dana's School of Dance, letting the conga line snake outside to the parking lot. Tables had been set up along the sidewalk. There were all kinds of refreshments—cupcakes, cake, pie, cookies, watermelon, strawberries, and lemonade waited for the hungry performers and their fans.

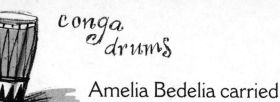
conga drums

ukulele

Spanish guitar

Amelia Bedelia carried the conga drum outside. Soon she was joined by Alex on the guitar and Alexandra on the ukulele. The beat was nutty and silly, but it was still music to Amelia Bedelia's ears. All of a sudden, she was reminded of her favorite show, *The World Is a Village*.

Amelia Bedelia was sorry the program was only in reruns these days. Their celebration would have made a great episode. There were dancers in amazing costumes, including Gracie with beautiful feathers under her arms, and giant flamingoes, and boys in grass skirts and colorful

kilts. There was a banquet with tasty homemade food.

Amelia Bedelia's father gave her a kiss on the top of her head.

"Hey, Bagel Bun," he said. "*Mmmmm!* You smell like my favorite deli."

"Oh, Daddy," said Amelia Bedelia.

"What did you slick back your hair with?" he asked. "Cream cheese?"

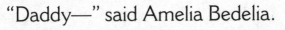

"Daddy—" said Amelia Bedelia.

"Okay, I won't tease," he said. "Your mother and I are proud of you."

Amelia Bedelia's mother grabbed Amelia Bedelia around her waist and

pulled her into the conga line. She leaned down and said, "We mean that. You were brave to take dance lessons. You never complained. Never missed a class. You tried something new, something different. You learned a lot and had fun. Your dad and I could not be more proud of you."

Amelia Bedelia stopped in her tracks. She turned around and hugged her mother.

"Family hug!" yelled Amelia Bedelia.

"Let me in on this," said her father.

"Hey, you three busybodies! Is there

room in there for one more?" It was Wanda, now bringing up the rear of the conga line.

Amelia Bedelia's father grabbed Wanda and pulled her toward them. "Extended family hug!" they all hollered.

Then the four of them just stood there in one big, sweet, long squeeze, letting the music and laughter fill their ears.

Amelia Bedelia's Wild World of Dance!

Ballet: Ballet is an artistic style of dancing that began long ago in Italy, France, and Russia. Ballets often tell stories with costumes and scenery (for example, *The Sleeping Beauty* or *The Nutcracker*), but ballets can also be a pattern of steps, usually set to music.

Break Dancing: Break dancing started in the US in the 1970s. It's often freestyle or improvised, with acrobatic moves similar to gymnastics. People sometimes call it breakin', b-boying, g-girling, or street dancing; it's part of hip-hop and is popular in movies and videos all over the world.

Ceremonial Dance: In many countries and cultures people dance to mark important events. A ceremonial dance, for example, might welcome a new baby or bring luck to the hunt.

Flamenco: Flamenco is a kind of folk dance that originated in Spain and is now taught all over the world. Guitar music, singing, foot stamping, hand clapping, and finger snapping can all accompany flamenco dance.

Interpretive: Most kinds of dance have set steps, patterns, beats, and movements but when you dance an interpretive dance you make up your own steps inspired by what you see, feel, smell, hear, or imagine.

Modern Dance: Modern dance originated in the US and Germany in the early 1900s. There are many kinds of modern dance, performed to many kinds of music, but typically a modern dancer has bare feet and dances with freedom and expression.

Polynesian Dance: Many dances originated in the Pacific islands of Polynesia (such as Tahiti, Tonga, and Hawaii). The hula dance comes from Hawaii and is known for the complicated and beautiful hand motions that accompany the words and music.

Rumba: Rumba is a form of ballroom couple dancing that originated in Cuba—now there are many styles and forms of rumba that are danced all over the world. The box step is a basic rumba form popular at parties and weddings.

Salsa: Salsa is danced for fun at social gatherings and parties. It began in New York City, probably in the 1970s, but the roots of the dance can be traced to Cuba, Puerto Rico, and other Latin American countries. There are many different styles of salsa, and it's almost always danced by two people.

Celtic Dancing: In Scotland and Ireland, dancers have been performing reels and jigs and other pattern dances for many years at parties, weddings, and other gatherings. Highland and Irish step dancers often dance alone and sometimes participate in big competitions. Famous Highland dances include the sword dance and the Highland fling.

Tap: Tap dancing is unique because the dancer uses shoes with metal plates on the soles to create rhythm and percussion. Tap dancing can be traced back to Ireland, England, and West Africa. There are two main kinds of tap dancing today—jazz tap and Broadway tap (the kind popular in movies and shows).

Dance on!

Two Ways to Say It
By Amelia Bedelia

"She could see a storm brewing."

"Glue your eyes to me."

"She could see trouble ahead"

"Pay close attention."

"You are a real busybody."

"She cleaned out the bank account."

"You are curious and bossy about things that are not your business."

"You have a lot on your plate."

"She spent a lot of money."

"You are incredibly busy!"

"Get some basic moves
under your belt."

"Learn and understand
the basics."

"Go with the flow."

"Relax, and don't let
anything bother you."

"Put your best foot forward."

"Do your very best."

"Break a leg!"

"Good luck with the
performance!"

"They are fossils,
just like us."

"They are very old,
just like we are."

☆ ☆ With Amelia Bedelia

#1

Amelia Bedelia wants a new bike—a brand-new shiny, beautiful, fast bike just like Suzanne's new bike. Amelia Bedelia's dad says that a bike like that is really expensive and will cost an arm and a leg. Amelia Bedelia doesn't want to give away one of her arms and one of her legs. She'll need both arms to steer her new bike, and both legs to pedal it.

Amelia Bedelia is going to get a puppy—a sweet, adorable, loyal, friendly puppy! When her parents ask her what kind of dog she'd like, Amelia Bedelia doesn't know what to say. There are hundreds and thousands of dogs in the world, maybe even millions!

#2

#3

Amelia Bedelia is hitting the road. Where is she going? It's a surprise! But one thing is certain. Amelia Bedelia and her mom and dad will try new things (like fishing), they'll eat a lot of pizza (yum), and Amelia Bedelia will meet a new friend—a friend she'll never, *ever* forget.

anything can happen!

#4

Amelia Bedelia has an amazing idea! She is going to design and build a zoo in her backyard. Better yet, she is going to invite all her friends to bring their pets and help plan the exhibits and rides.

#5

Amelia Bedelia usually loves recess. One day, though, she doesn't get picked for a team and she begins to have second thoughts about sports. What's so great about racing and jumping and catching, anyway?

#6

Amelia Bedelia and her friends are determined to find a cool clubhouse, maybe even a tree house, for their new club. One day they find the perfect spot—an empty lot with a giant tree. The lot is a mess, so they pitch in and clean it up. And that's when the trouble really begins.

Have you read them all?

#7 Amelia Bedelia is so excited to be spending her vacation at the beach! She loves hanging out with her cousin Jason—especially since he's really great at surfing and knows so many kids in town. But one night, Amelia Bedelia sees Jason sneaking out the window. Where is he going? What is he up to?

Amelia Bedelia does not want to take dance classes. She loves to dance for fun, but ballet is not her cup of tea, and she is sure that Dana's School of Dance will be super boring. But guess what? Surprising teachers, new steps, cool kids, and even a pesky ballet bun inspire Amelia Bedelia and her classmates to dance up a storm!

#8

#9

Coming soon!

Amelia Bedelia and her classmates are learning about jobs and occupations at school, and that means they go on some really interesting field trips. What does Amelia Bedelia want to be when she grows up? Turns out, the sky's the limit!